Little Chick's Breakfast

HarperCollins*Publishers*

An Early I Can Read Book®

Little Chick's Breakfast

Mary DeBall Kwitz

An Early I CAN READ Book

Pictures by Bruce Degen

This book is a presentation of Newfield Publications, Inc.
Newfield Publications offers book clubs for children
from preschool through high school. For further
information write to: **Newfield Publications, Inc.,**
4343 Equity Drive, Columbus, Ohio 43228.

Published by arrangement with HarperCollins Publishers.
Newfield Publications is a federally registered trademark of
Newfield Publications, Inc. I Can Read Book is a
registered trademark of HarperCollins Publishers.

Library of Congress Cataloging-in-Publication Data
Kwitz, Mary DeBall.
    Little chick's breakfast.

    (An I can read book)
    Summary: Little Chick becomes hungrier and hungrier
and more and more impatient as she watches all the other
barnyard animals getting their breakfast before she gets hers.
    [1. Chickens—Fiction. 2. Domestic animals—Fiction]
I. Degen, Bruce, ill. II. Title. III. Series.
PZ7.K976Lg 1983   [E]   82-48259
ISBN 0-06-023674-4
ISBN 0-06-023675-2 (lib. bdg.)

For Karen and her Little Chick
—M.K.

For Tzvi and Roy
—B.D.

"Wake up, Broody Hen,"

whispered Little Chick.

"I am hungry!"

7

Broody Hen took her head

from under her wing.

"It is not time for breakfast,"

said Broody Hen.

"Why not?" asked Little Chick.

"It is too early," said Broody Hen.

"It will be time for breakfast

when the sun comes up.

9

Now hush, my Little Chick,

and go back to sleep.

You will wake Red Rooster

and Speckled Hen."

Little Chick closed her eyes.

She sat very still.

But she could not sleep.

"I hope we have dried corn,"

said Little Chick.

"Dried corn is

my favorite breakfast."

Little Chick opened her eyes.

"I know," she said.

"I will watch

the sun come up."

Little Chick ran out of

the hen house.

The barnyard was dark

and quiet.

She sat down next to the fence
and waited.

The sky started to turn pink.

Little Chick heard Robin sing

his morning song.

She saw Red Rooster fly up

to the barn roof.

"COCK-A-DOODLE-DO!

SUN-UP! SUN-UP!"

crowed Red Rooster.

"WHERE? WHERE?"

shouted Little Chick.

She jumped up

and looked all around.

She could not see the sun.

But she saw a light go on

inside the barn.

Little Chick ran to the barn.

The farmer's daughter

was feeding the cow.

"Hay for the cow's breakfast,

Little Chick,"

said the farmer's daughter.

The farmer's son

was milking the cow.

"Milk for *my* breakfast,

Little Chick,"

said the farmer's son.

The cat walked into the barn.

"Meow!" said the cat.

The farmer's son laughed.

"And milk

for the cat's breakfast, too,"

he said.

"Where is my breakfast?"

asked Little Chick.

She ran out of the barn

to look for the sun.

21

She saw Speckled Hen

sitting in the tall grass.

"Speckled Hen," said Little Chick,

"are you waiting

for your breakfast?"

"No," said Speckled Hen.

"I am laying an egg

for the farmer's breakfast."

Speckled Hen stood up.

There lay one brown egg

in the tall grass.

The farmer's wife

came out of the hen house.

She was carrying a basket.

She put Speckled Hen's egg

in her basket.

Then she counted her eggs.

24

"One,

two,

three,

four.

Thank you, Speckled Hen,"

said the farmer's wife.

"Now I have four eggs

for breakfast.

One egg for the farmer.

One egg for the farmer's daughter.

One egg for the farmer's son.

And one egg for me."

"Everyone is getting breakfast

but me," said Little Chick.

Little Chick looked up at the sky.

The sun,

big and bright and orange,

was peeking over the barn roof.

"Now it is time

for my breakfast!"

cried Little Chick.

She ran around the barnyard.

"Broody Hen! Broody Hen!

SUN-UP! SUN-UP!"

"So it is, my Little Chick,"

said Broody Hen.

"And here is the farmer

with our breakfast.

Come, Little Chick,"

clucked Broody Hen.

30

Then Red Rooster,

Speckled Hen,

Broody Hen,

and Little Chick

walked all in a row,

pecking and eating

their breakfast.

"Hm-m-m!" said Little Chick.

"Dried corn

is my favorite breakfast!"